april is lush

a collection of poems by
aditya tiwari

© **Aditya Tiwari**
**2019 All rights
reserved**

All rights reserved by author. No part of this publication may be reproduced, stored in a retrieval system or transmitted in any form or by any means, electronic, mechanical, photocopying, recording or otherwise, without the prior permission of the author.

Although every precaution has been taken to verify the accuracy of the information contained herein, the author and publisher assume no responsibility for any errors or omissions. No liability is assumed for damages that may result from the use of information contained within.

First Published in March 2019

ISBN: 978-93-5347-349-5

Price: INR 299/-

USD 11.99

BLUE ROSE PUBLISHERS
www.bluerosepublishers.com
info@bluerosepublishers.com
+91 8882 898 898

Cover Design:
Pallavi Porwal

**Typographic
Design:**
Aditya Tiwari

Editor:
Apoorva Khare

Distributed by: Blue Rose, Amazon, Flipkart, Shopclues

*i just hope
you are everything
you believe in.*

april is the month of light, rediscovery, love, passion and balance

remember that some people like clouds will always try to diminish your brilliance but you like the sun should never stop shining

believe in yourself. there is magic in your veins.

it's time you realise it's all in you it's always been there all along

nothing or no one can stop you.

this book is for those who are termed as sensitive and sometimes too sensitive for this world because their hearts feel everything with a deeper intensity, and they've been beaten down so many times that they're just looking for a place where they can feel safe. this is for every person who is fierce, for every kid who felt they never belonged anywhere, for every child who is not accepted in their own home for being a part of LGBTQIA+, you are young, you are valid, you are loved, and accepted, celebrate yourself.

this is for you

my whole heart

- to the warriors

contents:

love

loss

trauma

LGBTQIA+

women

self-worth

as another beautiful
year has gone by
i kept wondering
to myself what did
 i do to deserve this

as i opened the
doors of my life
for you

and said forever
even when i knew

that forever
was a very long time
you shattered me
 within a blink of
an eyelash

whip lash

- late night thoughts and nostalgia

i can tell stories
from our past lives
where we were

sweet as sugar
and sour as grapes
together
like
romeo and juliet

i can tell
we were raw
like milk and honey
a perfect blend

- blended

i have been self-reflecting a lot today about my life and what i want out of it. thinking about my priorities. future. and how to stay at a great place mentally. i have not been well for the past couple of months and outgrowing some friends feels so good. i am glad that some friends made their exit. they will not be a part of my life anymore. i've left them behind. i've grown past them. and i am glad for the ones who keep me close. the new year is approaching with all its energy, all the timelines are in alignment. soak in everything and let all the old energies fade away / time to change. grow. and get better + letting all the old habits die young. and soak in warm energy. end of an era. loud noises. breathless moments. what a better time to be reborn again. this is my revival.
i have always questioned my power and tried to hide from others because i was too afraid. but i found that there is magic inside of me. i realized that the world is my oyster and i can do anything or become anything i want if i believe in myself. i was put on this earth filled with stardust, gold, and glitter, for a reason. and today i told myself little brown boy, there is magic in your veins. nothing or no one can stop you.

- voyage of self-reflection for next year

vaginas are the same from where you've come from.
breasts are the same
 from where your mum has fed you. when you were a
baby.
no keeping an eye on them. won't make you more of a
man.
 if she wears short clothes. no she won't be characterless.
if she will hang out
with guys. no she won't be a slut.

no every gay guy. doesn't want you. no every gay guy will
not get you girls
cause he's friends with them. remember when a girl says
no. a no is a no.
this is what. you need to know.

no every guy is not gay if he wears pink or shorts.
so dear men kindly have a broad perspective
cause it's 2019.

open your mind
and not
 your
 mouth.

- dear men

i have lived here
in my past life (a beautiful life)
but still it feels so
good to be back.

to a home
far away
from home

foreign land

- *diary of an immigrant*

say goodbye to the past
it's an unfinished
painting

create yourself all over again
you know you can do this.
become a new you. they don't
know you. only you know
you.

- you

you are emotional
you are sensitive
and you are powerful
you are enough but you've had
enough and you're just tired from
all the heartache. all the pain. all the chaos.
that now lives and breathes in your heart
and has now overtaken your mind
and you can't sleep because of it
but
i hope
you find rest
you deserve it.

- reflections

love tastes
like coffee
coffee tastes
so sweet

oh my beloved
when you
spilled the coffee
on my sheets
the stains lasted
forever

it didn't taste
so sweet
but bittersweet like violence.

- love's like coffee violence

all i wanted
wasn't love
anymore

i wanted a passion
because you told me
that i didn't have one
you were afraid of me
because you knew
i was fire.

you left me loveless
and shattered in
 pieces

i just want to
tell you that
 i am worthy
of everything
you said

 i couldn't be.

- *lovers like poison*

you like cigarettes
were not good
for my health

yet
i craved for
you
knowing that
you'd harm me

how weak of me to have not
controlled my urge
today we don't talk anymore
and

here
 i am
still living in
grief.

- *crave*

11:11 make a wish
does love to exist
in fairytales

you are always my 11:11 wish.
you have always been my
11:11 wish. till date you are
the only thing i ever ask for
when i look at a shooting star

you are still not here
and i am just living in
sorrow.

- 11: 11

be the man
she always wanted
you to be

she always longed
for a man
so strong
who could fix
all her
broken pieces

he never came
so that's what
 she became instead.

the man in the relationship

- *choices*

sometimes the past feels
like another lifetime
i am fading away
 so slowly
 you aren't even
noticing

and in those moments
when all i want to do is
 hide
my mind turns to
the shore
 and
 i breathe.

- if i just breathe

the void that you have right now
might be very haunting and dark
and it is because you have
 certain people blocking
your growth

choose yourself and nonetheless.

 it is very important for you
to preserve yourself. know that you
cannot continue watering a dead flower.

to all those who are in the greatest change of their lives - transitioning into a butterfly from a caterpillar. remember there are going to be people who will leave you at every moment you just got to remember they do not deserve you and let them go. if they don't deserve you at your worst they're surely not worth the best. the best is yet to come.

- finding yourself is a process

you've been holding onto a lot of unsolicited things
you must throw them out of the nearest window
in order to truly free yourself

freedom is power
and that is the greatest gift
you can give yourself + bloom in every valley
with love, understanding, and self-trust.

- dear self

april is lush

i have
 loved you
even when

 i didn't know
how to love
myself

but you
 taught me
how to do that.

the sad part is
 that i can see
you around
me

but i can't talk
 to you
because

i am afraid
you'd leave.

april is lush

what breaks my heart is
how you could not understand
me for me love is not just a word
it is pouring out of and into me.
love is embracing me and love is
what i embrace with.

i am worthy
of love

i don't deserve to
 be treated the
 way you treated
 me

after all these years
 i thought you'd
change but sad that
you had zero
growth.

men who rape women are cowards. men who bash gay people in the streets are cowards.
 men who rape lesbians are cowards. men who chase/harass trannies are cowards.
men who are egoistic and think they are the most superior and would do anything to prove it are cowards. men who hookup with 10 different girls at the same time and act to love them are cowards. men who teach themselves how to respect all diasporas of people from life are real men. be with someone who gives you love. compassion and warmth.

- dear men ii

i am not the same person i used
to be yesterday—therefore
i will not be
the same person i am today—tomorrow.

- *evolution*

april is lush

it takes guts to put your true-self

out there in front of   the world

stop judging people for who they are appreciate their confidence and empower each other.

beauty tip: fill yourself with light and love the others around you and remember you are awesome.

some days
love is like
 a sweet sadness

some days
love is a
 hurricane
on a
sunny day.

- mad love is a healer

april is lush

perhaps
my idea of love
 is very different
from your
 idea of
 love.

what makes
 you high?

tequila?

no
just love.

if god has given you the ability to help someone then you must do whatever it takes to give to those who are in need without expecting anything in return but only because it has come from the heart. remember not everybody is blessed with that.

- selfless

i believed in
you
even when

i didn't
believe in myself.

sometimes

i think that i have been strong for
so long that i'd break this very
moment
it's been a while since my ears heard the
echoes of someone saying i be there for you when
you fall.
but then (an angel said) i will always be there for you
no matter what and that was the most powerful thing
i heard in a while.

- friends out of strangers

like ghosts at 3:33 am
my wall clock stops ticking
they come into my life
from door to door
to haunt me and create
a passageway to leave.

- people who have left, ghosts

selfish people only come in your
life when they take a good look
at what you have to offer
and take and take away everything
till they leave you hollow and scattered in pieces.

- be careful who you forgive and invite back into your lives

she is a biological woman - closest to god because she is where life comes from. but i create my own life. i am no less than anything or anyone. because what i want to be is what i create of me. i have found the essence of being a woman within myself - empowered many like me and the generations after me. femininity is my most sensual weapon.

i am someone who has found and created the woman in me. i am more woman than any other woman. so, the next time you call me 'chakka' on the streets my soul will ache because i have changed my life from being who i used to be to who i am now which is not an easy path. my womb will hurt because of all the echoes of my unborn children. and my ovaries would bleed because i will never have periods like a normal woman.

i am no less than any other woman. when the red-hot-fierce lipstick hits my lips

i could set

a whole city

on fire.

- memoir of a transgender

we can't be friends
with you anymore
because if we do other children
will bully us too
you're a faggot deal with it.

- mean things i've been told as a child

they laughed at me
laughed at my clothes
laughed at the way i
spoke my broken english
with so much confidence
today all they want

 to do is become

like me
and that's my salvation.

- mean kids at school

april is lush

i gave you my heart
and you didn't know
what to do with it

so you ate

 it instead.

- *last day of love*

when you left

eyeliner and
cigarettes
became my best friends.

- give me eyeliner or give me death

you may think that your cigarettes are better than some people because they don't use and throw you like some people have in the past instead they let you use them when you need them and throw them when you are done. but my dear there's always a price to pay in the long run remember everything comes in twos just like life and death.

- stay away from your addictions

i still have
nightmares about
your hands
letting go of
 mine.

i said
 i am not letting you go
perhaps you should
see my broken heart
but you wrecked
me and
left.

- *stay i begged*

and
tonight i
won't sleep

i will be dressed
in moonlight
filled with
darkness

 waiting
for you.

- *blood moon*

april is lush

be careful
what you whisper
into the moonlight

angels are listening
 prayers are often
answered.

hold my hand
and save me
 from myself

because i am
 in a desperate
need of you.

april is lush

i am stronger
than my words
portray over here.

love me
till i find myself
 all over again.

after all these years

the last time
when i tried to
convince you

i gave up
on everything
and my heart
froze inside
my ribs.

- *cold heart*

the past is
filled with
so many ghosts.

- friends who made their exit

april is lush

no one

will

ever
take your
 place.

- *i'm lost in you*

even if the
door of my
heart is wide
open i can't
invite new
lovers in.

- my heart is haunted

of course
i will haunt
 your heart
you killed me
 there.

- *haunted house of heart*

you told me
that i wasn't good
enough for anyone

but baby
i have always
 been good
enough

 not for
 anybody else but
 for myself.

- i will love me if nobody else will

april is lush

what breaks me
over and over is
how you could
hold my hand and
lift me up the
staircase but you
chose to push me
down instead.

april is lush

i am right where
 i started because
 i reached on top—on top of you
 but you pushed me
 away.

april is lush

you think
i need a fixation?

i am beyond
 repair
  beyond beautiful.

be kind
always
always be kind.

i thought you'd lead
me home again on
a starry night but you lead me
to a road at midnight
that lead nowhere
and left me
there with
my sadness.

- *home with you*

i still remember
all the late night
 love. memories. and
magic. with you.

april is lush

i am leaving
my heart
 with you
 forever.

when love
becomes an
obsession
it eats you.

april is lush

the noise of
broken dreams
 is the loudest.

when you left
you took a part
of me
i was the
most proud of.

you told me
to tone it down
tone down my femininity
but how can i tone down
something
i was born with

 loving the feminine parts of me.

- *let boys be feminine, boys can be divas too*

maybe he is born with it
maybe he cares
maybe he doesn't.

you are a masterpiece
 no man could
 ever complete.

- *you're a piece of art*

sometimes the past only
feels like an unfinished
piece of art which
only you can
complete.

- *carver*

i used to think that
 i'd be nothing without you
 but i have always been me
long before i even met you.

- *recognition*

i loved you
like a thousand
drums played
just for one.

april is lush

surround yourself with
 people who empower you
love you for you and
 bring out the
 best in you.

maybe i am
 the truth

you're
 looking for.

- so blunt you can smoke the truth out of me

april is lush

love is such a strong word
understand the depth of
it. love is power. love is
magic.

words are very powerful
they cut like knives

 be careful what

you speak and who you
speak it to because

 once it's thrown out of
your mouth it can't be
reversed. all that's left is
grief.

april is lush

love me like a
hurricane

love me like the
thickest part
of a
thunderbolt

love me like
 you never
 did.

- *love storm*

the smell of first rain
makes me so nostalgic
about all the other ones
 and so many memories
attached.

- *deja vu*

how long
i have lived
 in fear

how long
i haven't
 lived.

- *pride*

some people teach you the depth of your heart by first ripping it to shreds and that's why you meet them these human shaped hurricanes these devastating beings disguised as soft flesh and bone tear you apart

you are young. you are valid. you are allowed to have dreams and achieve them. remember the world is your oyster. you can do anything. don't let the world put you down. get up ballerina. even if you fall. fall gracefully and recover.

- human shaped hurricanes

april is lush

i bend
but
 i do not break.

april is lush

you
are filled
with ashes
and you
like a phoenix
know how to
rise and resurrect.

when you accept yourself
for exactly who you are
you want to be the best version
of yourself you can be.
you don't need others to accept you.
acceptance leads to growth.

if you find yourself
in an environment or situation
that creates stagnation
love yourself enough
to leave.

your thought, words, and actions
are rapidly flowing
into your reality

this is an accelerated
time of manifestation
 in all areas
of your life.

change is the only constant
whatever you're dealing
 with currently good or bad
it too will pass.

 the secret to contentment is
to be ok with the ups and be ok with the downs.
life is always in a constant flow

when outside circumstances
can no longer shake
 your core
you stay rooted but flow.

april is lush

your stories disappear
in 24 hours
mine stay forever

how i have touched people
with my heart and
how deeply
i have touched
them.

i am in
darkness
and the
 gleam i seek
 is out of reach.

april is lush

love me
like everything
that ever went
 wrong was
worth it.

i want you
to pour all
your sadness
in me

and just
remember that
everything will
be just fine.

april is lush

i need
 you

in my
 life.

follow the voice
inside your

heart

it will
lead you
to the right
 place.

april is lush

i just want you
 to want me.

be my river

and heartbeat
to the everlasting
ocean.

april is lush

everything in life
 is so
temporary and transformable
you must
let it flow.

trust
      god
            always

- it's a process

april is lush

the right people
come into your
life when you

need them it's
wonderful and
it happens in so
many magical ways.

it's 2019,
people should now
understand that we
live in a world

where boys can
play princesses

and girls can
play soldiers.

surround yourself with people who value you and not your job or degree for them your success or failure shouldn't matter because at the end—all this means nothing. they should see you as you are and feel pride in your success and empower you in your failure. they are the real ones.

you will meet 10 different
people in life who will sit back
and clap but you need to recognize if
they the real ones they are the ones
who will clap when you succeed
but also clap when
you fail.

surround yourself with people
who shouldn't be concerned about
anything, but, you and only you - who truly love
you.

april is lush

everyone in the
world can doubt you
but if you believe in
yourself that's all you
will ever need to
reach your goals.

people come in and out
of your life only the
real ones
stay
preserve them. give them your time.
love. and compassion.

dreaming
is
endless

always remember that.

- *never stop dreaming*

never let any of your
bad experiences from the
past stop you from
moving forward.

- grow from the past towards the future

april is lush

open her thighs

and you'd see
the entire universe
within
strong enough
to
swallow you
whole.

- *the entire universe inside of her*

you think she's easy-breezy
and could become
 your best mistake
but baby she can turn from
 a soft breeze to a hurricane
which would blow
your existence.

- *blowing winds to hurricanes*

april is lush

some days
she is ganga
some days
she is kali

some days
she would
offer you
life

and some
days she
would simply
take it away.

- *god is a woman*

you think
she's fragile
and you can
touch her

but

when a woman
is on her worst
behavior
she could tear
up a town
in
two.

- don't confuse softness for weakness

april is lush

she is a woman
because she has
an entire universe
inside of her
too many milky ways - too many asteroid galaxies.

time heals
all things.

april is lush

she has claws

for breasts
and canines
for vagina
touch her and you'd be
ripped
to
shreds.

like a river

you should

never stop.

- *keep growing*

april is lush

some people look
better in the past
they shall not be
 welcomed in your today
it's important. you don't need them.

they are in the past for a
reason. even if they try to
reach out to you

beware. they are the ones who
will have a good look at what you
 have to offer **and** leave you empty.

sometimes the most pain is

caused by the ones we love
and that's why the pain is
there. it's all because we
love

try to love yourself today
and heal the deepest
 parts of you

if you can love them
you are capable to love yourself too
not everybody
can do that.

april is lush

every time
my phone rang
i thought it
was you

i wanted it
to be you

but i was
drowning and
you weren't
even listening.

every time
you said
something bad
to me

it was like i was
losing a part of me

you were slowly
plucking eyelashes,
taking out
fingernails. limbs.
heart. and everything.

april is lush

when you told me
that you love me
love me more than
sharks love blood
and then left me
with the void in me
and a frozen heart

and when after
all these years
you came back
and said that i
am like a
stranger to you

where did all
the love go

how naive of you
to not know that
i am a treasure box
full of love flowing
in and out of me.

- *love pouring in
and out of me*

dear little brown gay boy
you are enough. you have always
been enough.

never forget that.

- *the little boy with big dreams*

april is lush

some days
 i am soft
like a tidal wave

some days
i am the tsunami
 on a sunny day.

to me you are
 the entire
 universe
in human form.

don't confuse a
temporary state of mind
as a permanent
state of being.

- *good times are coming*

dear self

stay

strong.

april is lush

you are

the love

you are

the balance.

be soft
with me.

- soft like water

april is lush

and here

i am still
breathing

still trying to
fly each day
no matter how
hard i fall

because my
wings are injured
but not wrecked.

the road to
recovery is
a ruin

but in the
end

i'll meet you
where the
dead angels lie.

april is lush

your hands
unwrapped my
heart like a gift
on a christmas
morning.

people
empower
people

without each other
we are all nothing.

april is lush

always empower
and touch the people
around you tell them that
 they are loved and valid.

today when i see
the photos of you
or read old messages
of you my heart
starts bleeding.

- *wish you never left*

april is lush

it's important to give to others
sometimes it's not just the
materialistic things
all you can do is
give your time. love. and compassion.
to whoever needs it - give them warmth
and make them
feel loved.

- *unselfish*

men get eating disorders
men get raped
men self-harm
men get depressed
men get suicidal men commit suicide
it's not just the women
so to all the men
stay strong

i believe you. i believe that men are survivors too.

- *to all the men*

i have died
so many times
over and over
and yet again
like a phoenix
i am reborn again
this is my revival.

- a phoenix rises from the ashes

you and i all of us come from
the same place a mother who sees
all of us as one a mother who raises her
children to be warriors a mother who never
sees any disparity between her children irrespective
of their orientation or the color of their skin for her
you and i both are her children imagine when you
insult her children how does that mother feels

one morning i woke up and tried
to rub the brownness off me
and it didn't go away
that is when i realized
this is
who i am and
 i embraced it

yes i am brown
like the coffee
 that ignites you
every morning

yes i am brown
like the sizzling
brownie your
mouth waters for

april is lush

yes i am brown
like the nispero
you crave every
season

brown is what
i embrace with
and brown is what
embraces me

so the next time
you call me 'brown'
 know that
 yes i am brown
just like the

earth
 under
your
feet

and i am not
going anywhere.

- *brown*

lost girls always
 find their way.

april is lush

when love left
i locked myself in a
room full of darkness
pain and void i cried there for days
it was like i lost everything i lost a part of me
my eyelashes. fingernails. limbs. and everything.
but one day i gathered myself all together. loved
myself. and thanked god for everything. because if
you wouldn't have left i would not have nurtured
this love for my own self i washed yesterday's pain
from my hair. then love grew out of and into me. i
will never stop loving you. but this time i love me
too.

- i am no longer loveless

stop looking for love
let love find you and
when love finds you
love will play no
mind games

love give you warmth and light
love will fill you
with happiness

love will hold you and you will cry
and the grieving would fade away
love will teach you how to love yourself
all over again

wait for it and do not look for it in every corner. let love find you. one day it will come and when it does your life would change.

- stop looking for love

trapped inside a cage
like a prisoner
of love

human hearts
are
wild creatures

 - heart in chains

human hearts
are wild creatures
wanting to be loved.

april is lush

i just hope
that you believe
in yourself
even when other
 don't.

can u fix
my heart
can you ease
the ache
can you fix
the broken
pieces.

- *remedy*

april is lush

cracked heart
 in two need
a fixation.

staying out of reach

from people and cutting people off

has helped me in so many ways sometimes

all you need is yourself - and all you are

looking for to

save you is only you.

- *an avalanche of thoughts*

how am i supposed
to tell you things that
i am afraid of telling people
because when i show
my heart and spill it
it stains and people leave.

- fear

can we just
 switch our
souls

and do it
all over again.

april is lush

lungs crack at night
heartache so loud
that eats you
whole from
the inside.

ribs like cages
trapped heart
 inside

wanting to
break free.

- *wild heart*

april is lush

heart stains
 last forever.

give me your
good night kisses
and make me
fall asleep
this heart hasn't
rested a single day
since you've been
gone.

- *restless*

april is lush

little
 body

big
heart.

develop a thick skin
 over time
your lessons
make you stronger
and a
golden heart.

april is lush

some people have very little value
 of a human heart
 understand that the loss of a loved one
is not an easy thing
 it happens to all of us in so many unexpected and tragic ways
but
we live with it inside of us
we don't talk about it to everyone and live
with it in our daily lives. cry for days.
till it eats us whole from the inside
one by one makes our
 skin to bones and flesh to dust
it's one of the most life changing things understand
the depth of it
 and
love the others
around you.

- grief

april is lush

making flowers
 bloom from all
the pain
inside of me.

april is lush

all these years
i have just
 been growing
flowers
 inside of me

from all
 the pain that
 you gave me.

here's my
heart to you

and

obviously
 flowers.

- *first day of love*

did you even
turn back
and tried to see
how you
left me all in pieces—broken.

- *the fall out*

they say that
beautiful mosaics
are full of broken
 pieces

 i must be your
most beautiful
creation

because you
broke me too
 many times.

- *broken mosaics*

am i just dreaming
will i ever
find you now

- *dreams*

april is lush

healing comes from the inside
you can't help or heal people who have
 no interest in helping themselves light will
 only reach to you if you are willing to open the
curtains and let it in otherwise it's pointless.

april is lush

scream in my
 mouth and
 make flowers
bloom

inside the
 most desperate
 parts of me.

sometimes all you
 need to give people
is your love, time, and compassion.

april is lush

when everyone left
and the party
was over
i was drunk and
i found myself between
broken bottles of
champagne and glasses
that was the time when
poetry found me.

i crave for

red wine
long summer nights
romance
and
souvenirs
with you.

some days
i am the man
who will
hold you

and some days
i am the woman
who will
destroy you—tear you down.

- *androgyny*

i want to stay
connected with you
like a tree is
with its roots
because you
hold me down
and make me
 feel rooted.

- roots

april is lush

you probably
 just fell
 in and out
of love
 with me.

i am the strongest
 person but when
 i speak with you
 all my confidence
shatters.

april is lush

there have been people before you
generations ahead of you
who you can look up to
but did anyone tell you
little brown boy

that it takes immense
amount of strength to survive
and be who you want to be in a world
 where everybody just
wants to make you
 like the rest—ordinary.

- *queer brown representation*

maybe it's time
to fix that
broken heart

open up the
windows
and let
the healing
start

you know
who you are
let the fresh air
fill you with
life again.

april is lush

never give up
on love because
 even if it's
 one sided it
makes you
whole

perhaps gives
you wings and
in the end
love always wins.

you damaged
me
over and over.

april is lush

the road to love
is a long bumpy
road you must
die each day
to get to the top.

- *the journey*

i have been
lost for
 so long

i just need
 to be
found now.

do not let
weak men play with you
they only look better playing
with plastic dolls and you
 my dear aren't one

women like you
make such men drown
in them
you have a tsunami
inside of you
unleash it.

- tidal

some days i feel
like i will end up in
a psyche ward with all
my ex-lovers visiting me one by one
banging on the door with flowers in
one hand to greet me and a knife
 on the other
to plunge me.

- exes and psychos

the sadness is not going away
the healing won't start soon

nights become days. days
become nights flesh become
bones and bones become
dust.

this heart stopped beating
and the body cracked
in two.

- *remains*

i can't become this person
you're making me
you're making me transition
 into something i am not

i am not this person honestly
i don't even know who this person
is that i am becoming because of you

i had thought that you'd
make me feel home
i thought you were the only
 familiar thing i had known all along

but you shatter me
and tonight
i won't just grieve
i would shatter again
into a million pieces.

- *heartache*

after all these years
you don't know me
you don't know
how many stories
i have living
inside of me
yet you deny
 the existence
and truth of them.

- *growth*

do not speak to me
that way
you don't know me
anymore.

 - *strangers out of lovers*

i am not just
flesh and bones

i am a living being,
a life, space, zest.

 an entire universe.

april is lush

you could've
made me home
but you chose to
make me a hotel
room to rent
your happiness
for several hours.

the goddess
 inside of you
is screaming
tonight

she is angry
she wants to
 burn him alive.

- *hestia*

april is lush

i could never understand
why you chose to treat
me that way

maybe i was
too much
for you and you
didn't know what
to do with me.

april is lush

pride is living and breathing
freely cause this world has
already made it hard enough
for us how long we have lived in
fear how long we haven't lived.
our hearts know.

red wine
tastes like violence
with you.

april is lush

to the people from the past
who have bullied me
don't look at me with your hungry eyes
i am not a piece of meat for you to eat
i am not scared you anymore
you can't harass me anymore
you and i are no match you don't know me today
neither you did back then.
leave me alone.
i do not belong to you, i never have.
i am not just flesh and bones, i am a living being,
a life, space, zest. an entire universe, all in one.
i am an entire ocean that can
 give you life or drown
 you inside of me.

choose empathy.

april is lush

butterflies still make
love to abandoned
flowers.

the one you are
looking for is
'you'.

april is lush

all these years
brought all this
waiting

all this waiting
brought all this
fire and all this
burning.

- *expectations*

i wish you could
see what you've
done to me

ripped me to
pieces
skin and bones.

love
yourself
 first

- *reminder*

april is lush

stab me
in the heart
with flowers.

april is lush

no one
will ever
love you
like
i did.

april is lush

shouldve known
you'd make my
heart and brain
both collapse at the
same time.

april is lush

the universe
guides you in
so many different
and magical ways

you just have
to acknowledge it
and work your way
towards it.

please always believe in yourself and don't let anybody tell you otherwise. we all have our own inner battles going on. life has been hard enough already i just want you to know that better days are coming and will come eventually. all your struggles will fade away

believe in yourself. always.

april is lush

we have so many stories. personal struggles and inner battles. hidden inside of us. voices that can shatter a glass ceiling. we all empower each other without each other, we are all nothing. nothing or nobody can stop us, we're not going anywhere.

you become a passageway
between the two countries
motherland and foreign
land knowing too many
languages inside of you

trying to stay rooted to your
past and growing towards
your future too many
cuisines. cultures. dreams.
goals. and memories. inside
of you.

adaptations and hope for a
better future how can you
not be enough you have so
many stories living inside of
you no books can carry how
can you not become what
you want to be

 you are enough.

- immigrant

april is lush

love is such a strong word. understand the depth of it. love knows no gender. love knows no boundaries. it only knows that life has been hard enough already.

and
 in
the
end

love always wins. never forget that.

nobody warns
you about it

nobody tells you
to be prepare for it
it does not come
 with a warning
sign

it comes without
an explanation and
when it does
 it tears
you apart

you collapse and the thin
 line between life and death
starts to fade away.

- *depression*

nights become
 sleepless
days become
restless

in the night you
race like a
racing horse and
 in the day

you are
worlds apart.

- *nocturnal*

and remember
the truth can never
 be concealed

 and when
it comes out
it makes
 the loudest voices
so soft

and the
softer ones
more amplified.

you tell them
that you are
 fine

but these are
 just your
little lilac lies.

- *anxiety*

april is lush

when the night
cracks to the dawn
i think of you in my
darkest hours.

april is lush

i was told at the age of eighteen
that i would never be able to do
anything in future and i should listen
to them and do something i am not meant
to do but little did they know that i was put here
on this earth for a reason

in my twenties. here i am turning my pain—into
poetry—into art. for they have not known. that i
have just begun. it's just the beginning. the show
has just begun.

the real show
begins
in my thirties. i will age like old wine. the older. the
better.
my forties will be
like a tidal wave of ocean. and the party starts
at fifty
after midnight.

and i will only sleep when i am dead.

- *aging like old wine*

the reason why i am writing this book is not because i want it to be the best of the best. but because whatever little it is it will always be mine and nobody can take it away from me and that's my power. i was told at a very young age that i'd do nothing or i'd be nothing and here i am writing my heart out in this book. i come from nothing and i just want people to always believe in themselves and never let anyone tell them no for their dreams. last year was a year of so many challenges for me and i found myself. it's always these moments in life which show you who you are and what you are capable of overcoming. trust me, it's not easy, but i am proud of the person i am becoming.

as much as anyone can say how strong i seem, how fearless i am, or how brave i must be, i'm still human. i have seen things and dealt with more pain than some will deal with in their entire lives. but, i am still here, stronger each day, not just for myself, but for a greater purpose, because i feel like my story is far beyond me and it's for the world. because somebody out there really needs to see this. so, to anybody who isn't here to see how far i've gone or how far i've yet to go.

to friends i lost along the way, or maybe someone i gave my heart to who didn't know what to do with it.

this is for you

with love.

- acknowledgements

aditya tiwari is an indian-queer poet, writer, storyteller, and LGBT rights activist known for going beyond the boundaries.

moving to new york in 2016 to pursue a degree in journalism, aditya wasn't satisfied with being bi-cultural and realised that one had to be whole within the self — starting in 2014 with prose, and embracing poetry in 2017, it was clear when the party left, finding himself among some broken glasses and poetry, that he found his voice. however, you find your voice in an inspiration, from within you, describing poetry as breathing fresh air, self-expression, and an extension of his being, that lights his fire.

aditya raises his voice in alternating hushed and passionate tones of his poetry and asks you to do the same.

aditya released his first published book of poetry *'april is lush'* in april 2019 at the age of twenty.

- about the author

you can find aditya on:

instagram: @aprilislush

twitter: @aprilislush

Made in the USA
Monee, IL
03 May 2026